RAINBOW
magic®

The Music Fairies

sh

Special thanks to
Narinder Dhami

ORCHARD BOOKS
338 Euston Road, London NW1 3BH
Orchard Books Australia
Level 17/207 Kent Street, Sydney, NSW 2000
A Paperback Original

First published in 2008 by Orchard Books.

HiT entertainment

A CIP catalogue record for this book is available
from the British Library.

ISBN 978 1 40830 031 2
1 3 5 7 9 10 8 6 4 2

Printed in Great Britain by
CPI Cox & Wyman, Reading, RG1 8EX

Orchard Books is a division of Hachette Children's Books,
an Hachette Livre UK company

www.hachettelivre.co.uk

Maya
the Harp
Fairy

by Daisy Meadows

ORCHARD BOOKS

www.rainbowmagic.co.uk

I'm through with frost, ice and snow.
To the human world I must go!
I'll form a cool, Gobolicious Band.
Magical instruments will lend a hand.

With these instruments I'll go far.
Frosty Jack, a superstar.
I'll steal music's harmony and fun.
Watch out world, I'll be number one!

Contents

Confetti Surprise

"Isn't this a beautiful place for a wedding?" Kirsty Tate said as she and her best friend, Rachel Walker, bounded up the steps of the Wetherbury Hotel. Kirsty was carrying a large parcel wrapped in sparkly gold paper and tied with a silver bow, and Rachel's arms were full of pink flowers. Both girls were wearing pretty party dresses.

"Oh, *yes!*" Rachel agreed, glancing up at the old manor house, its stone walls covered in rambling ivy. "And the gardens are gorgeous too," she added.

The hotel was surrounded by emerald-green lawns and large beds of brightly coloured flowers, and there was a tall stone wall around the edge of the lawns with archways leading to the rest of the grounds.

"Isn't it brilliant that Kerry decided to have her wedding while you're staying with us for half term, Rachel?" Kirsty remarked as they paused at the top of the steps to wait for Mrs Tate. "That means you can come too!"

Rachel nodded. "It was nice of Kerry to invite us," she replied. "You must have been a *really* good little girl when she was your babysitter, Kirsty!"

Kirsty laughed. "Here's Mum," she said.

Mrs Tate was hurrying up the steps towards them. "Let's go inside, girls," she said, glancing at her watch.

"Kerry's expecting us to be early so we can help finish off the decorations for the wedding reception."

The doors into the hotel lobby stood wide open and Rachel gasped with wonder as they went in.

"Wow, this is *lovely*!" she exclaimed. The lobby was painted white and gold and there were huge vases of sweet-smelling roses everywhere. The carpet underfoot was thick, red and velvety, and a glittering glass chandelier hung from the ceiling. In one corner of the lobby was a man in a tuxedo, seated at a baby grand piano, leafing through sheets of music.

"Yes, it's perfect for a wedding, isn't it?" Mrs Tate agreed. "Girls, will you take the present into the reception room? I'll go and find Kerry. Oh, and Rachel, you give me the flowers and take these instead…" She handed a brown bag of confetti packets to Rachel. "Will you two scatter some of this confetti on the tables?"

"OK, Mum," Kirsty agreed, and Mrs Tate hurried off with the flowers. Meanwhile the girls went down a corridor to the reception room.

"What's that noise?" Rachel asked curiously as they got nearer to the open door.

"I don't know," Kirsty replied with a frown. "It sounds like a musical instrument, but it doesn't sound *right*!"

"Oh, I know!" Rachel exclaimed, "It's a harp. But it's very flat, and harp music is usually beautiful and light and airy."

"Well, we *know* why it doesn't sound right," Kirsty whispered. "It's because Maya the Harp Fairy's Magic Harp is still missing!"

Rachel nodded in agreement. The girls were helping their friends, the Music Fairies, to search for their missing Magical Musical Instruments, which made music fun and harmonious in both the human and fairy worlds. The instruments had been stolen by Jack Frost, who had sent his goblin servants to hide them in and around Wetherbury, ready for the National Talent Competition, which was taking place there at the weekend. Jack Frost and his goblins had formed a pop group called Frosty and his Gobolicious Band and they were determined to use the magic of the Music Fairies' special instruments to win the first prize, a recording contract with MegaBig Records. Rachel and Kirsty were very

worried that everyone in the human
world would find out about the
existence of Fairyland if Jack Frost
became a famous pop star.

"We still have three Magical Musical
Instruments to find before the talent
competition at the weekend," Rachel
reminded Kirsty as they went into the
reception room. "We must get them
all back – even if Jack Frost only has
one of the instruments, its magic will
help his band to win the competition!"

"I know," Kirsty
agreed, placing
the wedding
gift on a table
with a few
other prettily-
wrapped presents.

"We don't have much time left, do we?" She nudged Rachel. "Look, there's the harpist."

A woman in a long, silky, pink dress  was sitting at the other end of the room. She had a tall harp of polished wood in front of her and, with a frown, she plucked at a few strings as the girls watched. The sound of the harp was out of tune.

"Oh, hello," the woman called as she caught sight of Rachel and Kirsty.

"Sorry about the awful noise." She bit her lip. "I just can't seem to tune my harp at the moment. It sounds terrible! And I seem to be all fingers and thumbs today."

"Are you playing at Kerry's wedding?" asked Kirsty.

"Yes, I'm supposed to be playing *The Wedding March* for the happy couple," the woman went on, with a huge sigh. "But how can the bride walk down the aisle to *this* horrible noise?" She stood up, looking quite upset. "The wedding will be ruined if I can't sort out whatever's wrong!" she cried, and she rushed from the room in tears.

"Oh, what a shame," Kirsty said, dismayed.

"And poor Kerry too," Rachel added. "It doesn't look like she'll get her harp music after all."

"Well, at least we can make the room look lovely for her," Kirsty replied. "Let's decorate the tables, Rachel."

Rachel opened the bag. "There are lots of packets of pink and silver sparkly hearts," she said, taking one out.

"They'll look lovely scattered across these snowy-white tablecloths."

"And they'll match the gorgeous pink tulips," added Kirsty, glancing at the crystal vases of flowers that stood on each of the tables.

Rachel put the brown bag down on a nearby table and tried to rip open a packet of confetti. It was rather a struggle and in the end she had to use both hands to tug the packet apart. It burst open and the confetti flew out in a shimmering cloud of pink and silver sparkles. The girls were amazed as

the sparkles lingered in the air and then fizzed around the room in a flash of dazzling colours.

"Rachel, it's a *fairy!*" Kirsty cried.

Hunt the Goblin

As the sparkles began to fade, the fairy whizzed over to hover in the air in front of Rachel and Kirsty. She wore a floaty, halter-necked dress patterned with bright swirls of colour.

"Hi, girls!" she cried. "I'm Maya the Harp Fairy!"

"Oh, hello, Maya," Rachel exclaimed in delight. "Is your harp somewhere close by?"

Maya nodded. "Yes, and the goblins are too!" she said, twirling down to rest lightly on the white tablecloth. "We must find my harp, girls, or Kerry's wedding will be ruined!"

"Let's start looking for the goblins right away," Kirsty began, but Rachel pointed at the brown bag of confetti packets.

"We'd better do this first or your mum won't be too pleased, Kirsty!" she said with a grin.

"My magic can do that in a flash," Maya chimed in. She pointed her wand at the bag and instantly, in a shower of fairy sparkles, all the packets of confetti flew out. They hovered in the air for a second and then burst open with a pop. A huge cloud of glittering pink and silver hearts whirled around the room, scattering themselves across the white tablecloths.

"Perfect!" Kirsty laughed as the last few hearts settled neatly into place.

"Now we can go on a goblin hunt!" Maya said with a smile. "Remember, girls, that Jack Frost has given the goblins a magic wand to change the size of the Magical Musical Instruments. And his spell has also made the goblins little-boy-sized and flesh-coloured, not

green. So they'll be able to blend in
with the wedding guests."

"Yes, but the spell didn't work
completely, so they still have big noses,
ears and feet!" Kirsty added.

Rachel reached over and took a pink
tulip from one of the vases.

"You can hide in here, Maya,"
she said.

Maya flew over to the tulip and
slipped between the silky pink petals,
out of sight.

"Let's go, girls!" she
whispered.

"Where shall we start
looking, Rachel?"
asked Kirsty as they
went out into the
corridor.

"Let's go back to the lobby and start from there," Rachel suggested.

As the girls made their way back to the lobby, Rachel carrying the tulip, a man in a tuxedo came hurrying towards them. He looked very annoyed and was mumbling to himself.

"Really, that's no way for one musician to treat another!" he muttered furiously. "I shall complain to the hotel manager."

The man was so angry, he barged right past the girls and almost knocked Maya out of the tulip. She just managed to grab hold of a petal to stop herself from falling.

"Are you all right, Maya?" asked Kirsty, when the man had disappeared around the corner.

Maya popped her head out of the tulip and nodded.

"I wonder what's the matter with *him?*" said Rachel.

"I think it's the piano player from the lobby," Kirsty replied. "Remember? He was about to start playing when we arrived."

"Listen!" Rachel grabbed her friend's arm. "I can hear music!"

Maya and the girls listened. They could all hear ripples of sweet, airy music coming from the lobby just ahead of them.

"That's my harp!" Maya gasped.

Kirsty and Rachel ran towards the lobby. It was packed with people listening to the beautiful music, and it was so crowded, the girls couldn't see Maya's harp or the harpist.

"What shall we do?" Kirsty whispered to Rachel.

"We'll just have to push our way through the crowd as politely as possible!" Rachel whispered back.

The girls began to weave their way through the lobby, Rachel still holding tightly onto Maya's tulip.

"Excuse me," Rachel said politely to an elderly woman who looked completely entranced by the music. "Can you let us past, please? We want to see who's playing the harp."

"Of course, my dear," the woman replied, moving aside a little. "Isn't it amazing to see such a young boy playing so beautifully?"

Rachel and Kirsty exchanged a glance. Now they could see the harpist, plucking at the strings of a beautiful golden harp. He wore a suit with tails and a top hat, but these couldn't disguise his big nose, ears and feet.

"It's a goblin!" whispered Kirsty.

Musical Statue

The goblin drew his fingers across the strings with a final, rippling flourish and the audience broke into rapturous applause. Grinning, the goblin stood up and swept his top hat off in a low bow.

"Do you think he's going to play another piece?" Rachel asked Kirsty.

"I hope not," Kirsty replied, "because we've no chance of getting Maya's harp back with all these people around!"

The goblin was about to seat himself at the harp again when the crowd suddenly parted to let  through a tall man, wearing a badge which read "Hotel Manager". Close behind him was the piano player, still looking very annoyed.

Kirsty and Rachel watched as the hotel manager went up to the goblin.

"Thank you very much for your lovely performance," he said with a strained smile. "It was completely unexpected, but everyone enjoyed it. However, it's the piano player's turn to perform now."

The goblin looked outraged. "I'm a *much* better musician than him!" he snorted. And, sticking his tongue out at the hotel manager and the piano player, he grabbed hold of the harp and wheeled it away.

"After him!" Maya whispered from her tulip.

Rachel and Kirsty hurried after the goblin, weaving their way in between the crowd of people which had now begun to disperse.

"He's leaving the hotel!" said Kirsty, just catching a glimpse of the goblin wheeling his harp out of the main entrance.

The girls went after him as fast as
they could, but it was difficult with so
many people still around. More guests
were arriving for the wedding, too, and
it was a few moments before Rachel
and Kirsty could get out of the main
doors.

"We've lost him!" Rachel
exclaimed in dismay.

"No, there he
is!" Kirsty cried,
pointing across
the gardens.

The goblin
was just
disappearing
through
one of the
ivy-covered archways.

Maya fluttered out of the tulip and she, Rachel and Kirsty raced after him. They peeked through the arch and saw the goblin pull an icy wand out from inside his jacket. He pointed it at the harp and it shrank down to pocket-size in the blink of an eye.

"Let's try to grab the harp!" Rachel suggested.

The three friends dashed through the arch, but the goblin heard their footsteps. He spun round with a shriek of rage.

"Go away, pesky girls!" he roared, snatching up the tiny harp. He slipped it into his pocket and ran off towards another archway.

Rachel, Kirsty and Maya followed. On the other side of the arch was a beautiful rose garden with marble statues of Greek gods. But the goblin was nowhere to be seen.

"He must be here *somewhere!*" Kirsty panted. "Because there's no other way out!"

Maya and the girls began to search the rose garden. They looked behind every rosebush, but there was no sign of the goblin anywhere.

Suddenly Rachel clutched Kirsty's arm.

"Look," she said in a low voice. "See that statue under the willow tree at the bottom of the garden?"

Kirsty looked where Rachel was pointing. There was a tall stone wall at the bottom of the rose garden, and next to it was a willow tree. Under the tree stood a marble statue of a woman in a flowing robe. The statue, which was placed on top of a high plinth, was in shadow, half-hidden by the willow's long, drooping branches.

"The goblin could be hiding under the willow tree!" Rachel went on.

"Let's go and see," Maya said eagerly.

The three friends hurried over to the tree, and Rachel began to part the branches carefully, searching for the goblin.

Meanwhile, Kirsty glanced up at the tall statue. Suddenly she caught a very quick glimpse of a top hat before it whisked out of sight again.

The goblin's hiding behind the statue!

Kirsty thought. *He must have climbed up onto the plinth!*

She glanced at Maya and Rachel, then put her finger to her lips and pointed at the statue. They nodded in understanding.

"The plinth's quite high," Kirsty whispered. "Rachel, if you stand on my shoulders, do you think you'd be able to get the harp out of the goblin's pocket?"

"I'll try!" Rachel whispered.

Quietly the three friends made their way over to the base of the statue. But before they could carry out their plan, they heard a shriek of fury high above their heads.

"Look out! Horrible girls *and* a dratted fairy!"

Dismayed, Maya, Rachel and Kirsty looked up and saw a second goblin sitting on top of the garden wall. He reached down behind the statue and grabbed the goblin with the harp, hauling him up onto the wall.

"Ha ha!" the goblins jeered, pulling
faces at Maya and the girls. "We win
and you lose! You'll never get the
Magic Harp back now!"

And with that, they disappeared over
the garden wall.

Trolley Trouble

"Oh no!" Rachel exclaimed. "How are we going to catch them now? The wall's too high for us to climb over."

"The wall isn't a problem," Maya replied with a smile, "if you have wings!"

She flew over the girls' heads, showering them with a cloud of multi-coloured fairy sparkles from her wand.

Immediately Rachel and Kirsty became
fairy-sized, with the same glittering
wings as Maya's on their backs.

"Here we go!" Maya cried, linking
arms with the girls.

Together all three of them soared up
and over the wall.

"There go the goblins!" Kirsty
shouted, catching sight of them in the
distance.

"And it looks like they're heading back towards the hotel!" Rachel added. The goblins were running back across the lawns to the hotel entrance.

"I bet there are lots of people inside now, because all the wedding guests will have arrived," said Kirsty, as the goblins dashed into the lobby. "The goblins are probably hoping that they'll be able to hide themselves in the crowd!"

"We must be careful not to get spotted, girls," Maya said anxiously.

Rachel, Kirsty and Maya flew into the lobby. As Kirsty had guessed, it was now packed with people. The girls and Maya kept as close to the edges of the room as possible to avoid being seen by the guests.

47

"There are a lot of fancy wedding hats around!" Rachel gasped, as she zipped upwards to dodge a large-brimmed, pink straw hat.

"Let's fly higher and check out what's happening," Maya said in a low voice, pointing up at the crystal chandelier. They all whizzed upwards and perched among the sparkling droplets of glass.

"There are so many people here,"
Kirsty remarked, staring down at the
wedding guests. "The goblins could be
anywhere!"

Rachel grinned. "I think I see one of
them!" she said. "Look at that waiter!"

Kirsty and Maya saw a waiter below

them. He looked rather
odd because his jacket
was too big and came
right down to his
knees. He was
pushing a trolley
with a beautiful,
white, four-tiered
wedding cake on it.

"It's the goblin who was on top of the
wall!" said Maya. "But where's the
goblin with my harp?"

"Look at the bottom shelf of the trolley!" Kirsty laughed.

The trolley was covered with a long

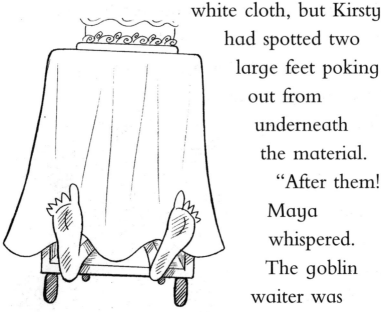

white cloth, but Kirsty had spotted two large feet poking out from underneath the material.

"After them!" Maya whispered. The goblin waiter was wheeling the trolley towards the reception room as fast as he could through the crowd.

"I hope the goblins are careful with Kerry's cake," Kirsty said, frowning, as they flew after them. "It would be awful if anything happened to it!"

As the goblin pushed the trolley into the reception room, Maya, Rachel and Kirsty ducked inside too. They just managed to hide behind the sparkly bow on top of one of the wedding presents before the goblin closed the door.

"You can come out now," the waiter said triumphantly to the other goblin. "We've managed to dodge that silly fairy and her human friends!"

The goblin with the harp climbed out
from under the tablecloth, grinning
gleefully. But suddenly the door swung
open and a woman in a
pretty, rose-pink suit
and a white hat
hurried in.

"Oh!" Kirsty
whispered. "It's
Kerry's mother,
Mrs Bolton!"

Mrs Bolton
was looking
annoyed.
"Oh,
you've
brought the
cake at
last!" she exclaimed. "We were

beginning to wonder where it was."

The goblins looked rather sheepish.
"Well – er –" the goblin waiter began.

"Oh, never mind that now," Mrs
Bolton said impatiently. "Put the cake
on that table in the corner, and *do*
hurry up!"

The goblins rushed to pick up the
cake as Mrs Bolton went out again,
closing the door behind her.

"Oh, I can't look!" Kirsty groaned,
covering her eyes. The girls and Maya
held their breath as the goblins lifted
the cake off the trolley and placed it
clumsily on the table.

"At least the cake's safe!" Rachel said with a sigh of relief. "Now it's time to get the harp! But how?"

A Wrestling Match

"Any ideas, girls?" asked Maya.

Kirsty and Rachel both thought hard. Meanwhile, below them, the goblins were smirking, looking very pleased with themselves.

"I'm going to play at the wedding!" the goblin with the harp announced proudly. "I'm a *much* better player than that human woman. Her harp sounded all flat and horrible!" And he took Maya's harp out of his pocket and stroked it lovingly. The second goblin looked on enviously.

Kirsty grinned. "If there's one thing we can always count on, it's the goblins arguing with each other!" she whispered. "Maybe we can get them to argue over the harp?"

"Great idea, Kirsty!" Rachel agreed. "And while they're disagreeing, Maya can swoop down and get it back,"

"Go for it, girls!" said Maya.

Rachel and Kirsty flew across to the goblins. Rachel zoomed towards the goblin who had the harp while Kirsty hurried over to the other one.

"Oh no!" shrieked the goblin furiously when he saw Rachel. "Fairies!"

"I just wanted to tell you something," Rachel said quickly. "I've noticed that other goblin looking at your harp. I'm sure he's going to try to steal it from you!"

The goblin frowned. "I'd like to see him try!" he muttered.

Meanwhile, Kirsty was talking to the second goblin.

"Why don't *you* have a go at the harp?" she said. "I'd like to hear how *you* play."

The goblin looked very sulky.

"*He* won't let me," he grumbled, pointing at the first goblin.

Kirsty pretended to look astonished. "Doesn't he *ever* share?" she asked.

The second goblin shook his head. "No, he's mean!" he replied.

Kirsty tutted and said, "I don't think you should let him get away with that!"

"You're right," said the second goblin. "Well, he's going to share *now*!" And he dashed across the room and tried to grab the harp from the other goblin.

"Get away!" the first goblin howled, giving him a shove. Next, the two goblins were rolling around on the floor, wrestling over the harp!

Kirsty and Rachel hovered nearby as Maya fluttered down, looking for an opportunity to grab the harp. But it was difficult for her to get close to the fighting goblins.

"Oh no!" Rachel gasped as the goblins rolled towards the table with the wedding cake on it.

"Maybe this wasn't such a good idea of mine after all!" Kirsty said anxiously.

The goblins bumped into the table leg and the wedding cake began to wobble dangerously.

"The cake's going to fall!" Kirsty cried.

"Maya, HELP!" Rachel shouted.

Maya glanced up, saw the cake beginning to topple, and instantly waved her wand. A stream of magic sparkles swirled towards the cake and surrounded it, keeping it upright.

Kirsty breathed a sigh of relief. But just at that moment, the second goblin managed to knock the tiny harp from the first goblin's hand. Maya, Rachel and Kirsty watched in dismay as the harp sailed through the air.

"It's heading straight towards the wedding cake!" Rachel gasped.

Before Maya and the girls could do anything, the harp landed right in the middle of the top tier of the cake.

"At least the harp is tiny, so it won't have done any damage to the cake," Maya reassured the girls. "Now let's grab the harp before the goblins do!"

The goblins had dashed over to the table and now both were standing on tiptoe trying to reach the harp. But as Maya, Rachel and Kirsty flew towards the cake, the door suddenly opened again. Maya grabbed the girls' hands and pulled them behind one of the vases of tulips, just as a girl wearing a pink silk dress and a beautiful flower in her hair breezed into the room.

"That's Kerry's bridesmaid!" Kirsty whispered. "Isn't her dress gorgeous?"

"Oh, do leave that cake alone and come and help me!" the bridesmaid told the goblins with a smile. "There's still *so* much to do." She glanced at the cake and then gave a gasp of delight. "Oh, Kerry will *love* that harp decoration – it's the perfect finishing touch!"

She turned to the goblins. "Follow me," she ordered, grabbing their hands and pulling them over to the door.

"You can collect the gifts from the guests before the ceremony begins and put them on the table over there."

The goblins glanced anxiously at the harp but they couldn't take it with the bridesmaid looking on. Maya, Rachel and Kirsty laughed quietly as the bridesmaid ushered the reluctant goblins out of the room.

"Come along," she said bossily. "The wedding's starting soon and we've got work to do!"

Here Comes the Bride

As soon as the bridesmaid and goblins had left the room, Maya flew over to the cake and picked up her harp. She drew her fingers gently across the strings, filling the room with magical music.

"The cake *did* look lovely with the harp on top," said Kirsty. "It's a shame it won't have one now."

Maya smiled. As her harp transformed back to its Fairyland size she began to play a different melody, and as she did so, a glittering spiral of fairy sparkles began to spin around the top tier of the cake. As Rachel and Kirsty watched in wonder, they saw the top of the cake shimmer and glow.

"Look, Rachel!" Kirsty cried. "There's a *new* harp on the cake!"

"And it looks exactly like Maya's," Rachel added.

"It *looks* exactly the same but there's one big difference." Maya pointed her wand at the harp on the cake. "This one is made of marzipan, so you can eat it!"

The girls laughed.

"What's that?" Rachel said suddenly, as she heard the faint sound of sweet music in the distance. "It sounds like *another* harp."

"The wedding's starting!" Kirsty exclaimed.

Quickly Maya sprinkled the girls with fairy dust so that they instantly grew back to their normal size.

"Thank you for everything!" Maya said. "Now I must take my harp back to Fairyland, and *you* must go to Kerry's wedding!"

And, with a wave, Maya vanished
in a mist of glittery sparkles.
Following the sound of the harp, Kirsty
and Rachel rushed to the large hall
where the wedding was being held.
They could see the harpist playing at
the front of the hall.

"Here comes Kerry!" Kirsty whispered
as they sat down next to Mr and Mrs
Tate. "We were just in time!"

Beaming, the girls watched as Kerry, looking lovely in a long ivory satin wedding dress, walked down the aisle to the melodious sound of the harp.

"The harp sounds beautiful, doesn't it?" Rachel sighed happily.

"Because the Magic Harp is back in its proper place in Fairyland!" Kirsty replied. "We only have Victoria's violin and Sadie's saxophone to find now!"

RAINBOW
magic ®

Rachel and Kirsty must now help

Victoria the Violin Fairy

Can Rachel and Kirsty help Victoria
to find her Magic Violin before Jack
Frost and his Gobolicious Band win
the National Talent Competition?

Listen to the Band

"I like that song," Rachel Walker said, pointing at the computer screen. She and her best friend Kirsty Tate were downloading music from the internet, using a gift card that Rachel got for her birthday.

Kirsty nodded. "Me too," she said, clicking the mouse to download the track. Rachel was staying with Kirsty's family for a week over the autumn half term, and so far the girls had been having a very exciting time. A very *musical* time, too – helping the Music

Fairies find their lost Magical Instruments!

Mr Tate, Kirsty's dad, came into the room at that moment. "I've just been talking to my friend Charles on the phone," he told them. "Kirsty, do you remember him? He works at Wetherbury College and he's been telling me about a really talented band who have been practising there. He's sure they're going to do well in the National Talent Competition tomorrow."

Kirsty's ears pricked up at her dad's words. She and Rachel knew someone else who was determined to go far in the National Talent Competition – Jack Frost! He was so desperate to win the contest he'd ordered his goblin servants

to steal the Music Fairies' Magical
Instruments so that his group, Frosty
and his Gobolicious Band, would sound
the best. Jack Frost wanted the star prize
– a recording contract with MegaBig
Record Company – but Kirsty and
Rachel knew this would be a disaster.
Once the public discovered that Jack
Frost wasn't human, all the girls' fairy
friends would be in danger of being
discovered by curious humans!

Win Karaoke Machines and Dance Mats!

Have you ever wanted to be a top musician like
Ellie the Guitar Fairy or a dancing queen like
Tasha the Tap Dance Fairy? Now's your chance
to shine like a star!

We have 5 Karaoke Machines and 5 Dance Mats
to give away in our special Rainbow Magic competition*.
All you have to do is answer the questions below:

What is the name of the fairy in the
first Rainbow Magic book?

Complete this sparkly sentence in 25 words or less.
I love Rainbow Magic because...

Send your entry on a postcard to
Rainbow Magic Karaoke Competition, Orchard Books,
338 Euston Road, London NW1 3BH

* Closing date: 31st December 2008. 5 winners will be drawn
at random and notified by 30th Jan 2009. For terms and
conditions please see **www.hachettechildrens.co.uk/terms**

Look out for the

Magical Creature Fairies!

Available
April 2009

CAITLIN
THE ICE BEAR FAIRY
978-1-40830-355-9

LEONA
THE UNICORN FAIRY
978-1-40830-354-2

SOPHIA
THE SNOW SWAN FAIRY
978-1-40830-353-5

RIHANNA
THE SEAHORSE FAIRY
978-1-40830-352-8

ERIN
THE FIREBIRD FAIRY
978-1-40830-351-1

LARA
THE BLACK CAT FAIRY
978-1-40830-350-4

ASHLEY
THE DRAGON FAIRY
978-1-40830-349-8

The Music Fairies

Win Rainbow Magic goodies!

In every book in the Rainbow Magic Music Fairies series (books 64–70) there is a hidden picture of a musical note with a secret letter in it. Find all seven letters and re-arrange them to make a special Music Fairies word, then send it to us. Each month we will put the entries into a draw and select one winner to receive a Rainbow Magic Sparkly T-shirt and Goody Bag!

Send your entry on a postcard to Rainbow Magic Music Fairies Competition, Orchard Books, 338 Euston Road, London NW1 3BH.
Australian readers should write to Hachette Children's Books, Level 17/207 Kent Street, Sydney, NSW 2000.
New Zealand readers should write to Rainbow Magic Competition, 4 Whetu Place, Mairangi Bay, Auckland, NZ.
Don't forget to include your name and address.
Only one entry per child.
Final draw: 30th September 2009.

Good luck!

Have you checked out the

website at:
www.rainbowmagic.co.uk